one mitten

ISBN-13: 978-0-439-02453-2
ISBN-10: 0-439-02453-6

Text copyright © 2004 by Kristine O'Connell George.
Illustrations copyright © 2004 by Maggie Smith. All rights reserved. Published by Scholastic Inc., 557 Broadway, New York, NY 10012, by arrangement with Clarion Books, a Houghton Mifflin Company imprint. SCHOLASTIC and associated logos are trademarks and/or registered trademarks of Scholastic Inc.

24 23   14 15 16 17/0

Printed in the U.S.A.   40

First Scholastic printing, January 2007

The illustrations were executed in acrylic gouache.

The text was set in 20-point Italia Book.

one mitten

by Kristine O'Connell George • Illustrated by Maggie Smith

SCHOLASTIC INC.
New York   Toronto   London   Auckland   Sydney
Mexico City   New Delhi   Hong Kong   Buenos Aires

One mitten,
yellow and bright,
fits on my left hand . . .

5

or on my right.

One mitten can wave
a mitten hello.

PIGS

9

One mitten can make
a shadow show . . .

with shadow shapes
of a mitten whale

and a slow, slow
mitten snail.

11

One mitten is a hat
for a rooster's head,

or a very small
mitten-bag bed.

One mitten
is a mitten flag.

"Hold still, Daisy . . ."

"Wag, Daisy, wag!"

One mitten gives my sleepy cat
a kitten-soft one-mitten pat.

And, under the cat, some yellow fuzz . . .

My other mitten!

So that's
where it was!

Two mittens can clap,

flap mitten wings,

make mitten ears—

21

lots of
two-mitten things.

22

Two mittens windshield-wipe
the frosty glass.

It's snowing outside,
covering up the grass!

25

Two mittens make binocular eyes.

Two mittens wave
mitten goodbyes.

27

Then, one mitten,
yellow and bright,
holds my friend's hand
warm and tight.

29

Two friends with mittens,
we're ready to go—

skipping, mitten-warm,
into the snow.

31

For the Colorado cousins
—K. O. G.

For Zoë and Isobel
—M. S.